FROGGIE WENT A-COURTING

You are cordially invited
to celebrate the wedding
of Mr. Frog and Ms. Mouse
next Saturday night
around seven
in the crown of the
Statue of Liberty
in New York Harbor,
New York, New York.

dinner & dancing to follow

by Marjorie Priceman

LB
1837

Little, Brown and Company
Boston   New York   London

For Megan, who had the idea

First Edition

Library of Congress Cataloging-in-Publication Data

Priceman, Marjorie.
    Froggie went a-courting / Marjorie Priceman — 1st ed.
        p.   cm.
    Summary : An updated version of the familiar folk song about the courtship and wedding of Frog and Ms. Mouse, set in New York City.
    ISBN 0-316-71227-2
    1. Folk songs, English — United States Texts.   [1. Folk songs — United States.]   I. Frog he would a-wooing go (Folk song)
II. Title.
PZ8.3.P923Fr 2000
782.42162'13'00268 — dc21   99-25703

10 9 8 7 6 5 4 3 2 1

TWP

Printed in Singapore

The illustrations for this book were done in cut paper and gouache.
The text was set in Cantoria Semibold, and the display type
was hand-lettered by Marjorie Priceman.

ABOUT THIS STORY

This book is based on a folk song written in Scotland
more than four hundred years ago. Many versions exist,
and for years children all over the world have enjoyed singing
it and making up verses of their own. This tale is set in
present-day New York City. Although every version of the
song is unique, each celebrates the wedding
of two very different creatures:
a frog and a mouse!

Froggie went a-courting, he did ride
A taxicab to the Upper West Side.

Jumped out at Ms. Mouse's place,
Anticipation on his face.

Frog got down on bended knee,
Said, "Ms. Mouse, will you marry me?"

Mousie nodded her consent.
White lights announced the big event.

Then Auntie Rat cried, rushing in,
"You cannot marry an amphibian!

A slimy frog—he's not our kind!"
But Mousie had made up her mind.

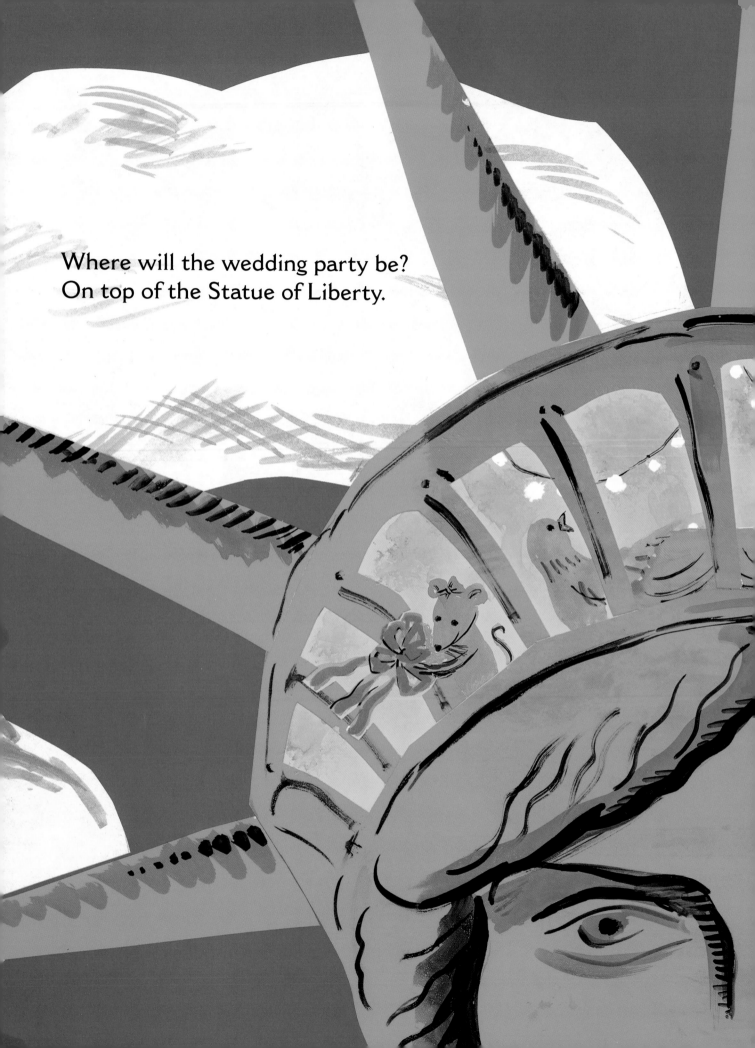

Where will the wedding party be?
On top of the Statue of Liberty.

Who will make the wedding gown?
Ms. Dragonfly in Chinatown.

How many layers for the cake?
As many as floors in the Empire State.

Auntie Rat shook her head.
"This wedding must be stopped!" she said.

But, into town the guests did funnel.
Some by bridge and some by tunnel.

First to come were a pair of fishes.
They set out the dinner dishes.

Next to come were a bunch of bees,
Played some jazzy melodies.

Third to come was a bushy squirrel,
Took Ms. Sparrow for a whirl.

Mr. Katydid came fourth,
With Ladybug and Gypsy Moth.

Finally came spotted Snail,
Then came a guest with a long black tail.

The tail belonged to a big tomcat.
He ran after Auntie Rat.

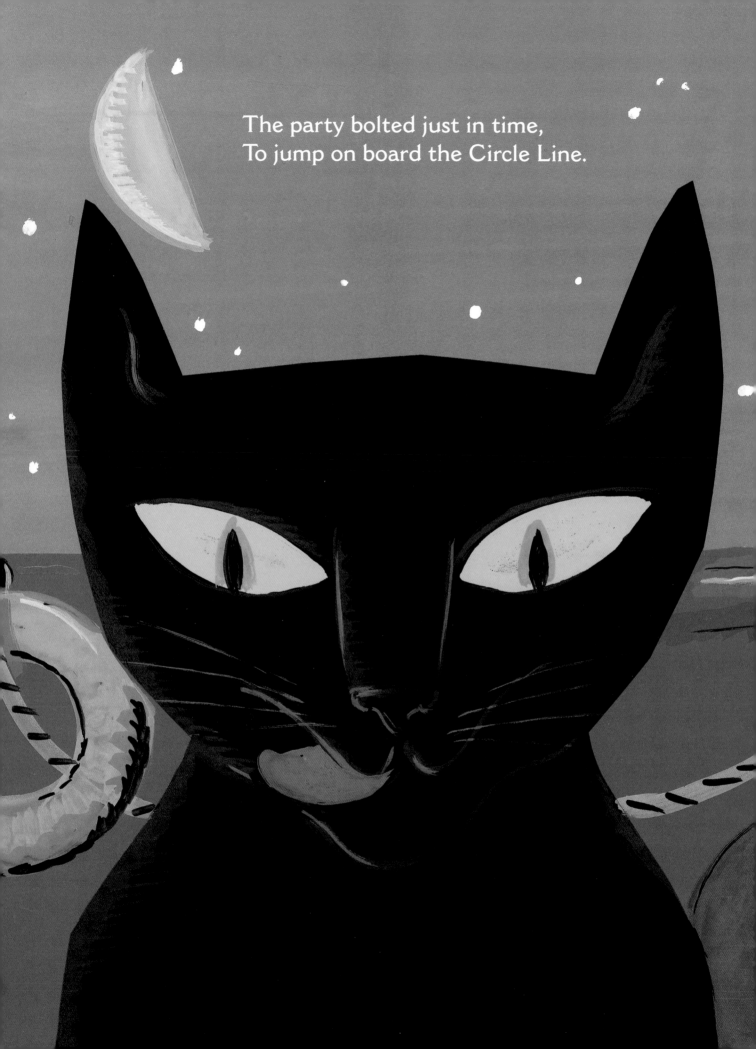

The party bolted just in time,
To jump on board the Circle Line.

For Auntie Rat they all did cry.
A speech was made by Firefly.

"Though Cat ate rat, there's no denial,
Aunt Rat at last made someone smile."

So Pigeon turned to navigating.
All resumed their celebrating.

Bees picked up their horns to play.
Ladybug caught the bride's bouquet.

The cake was cut, a toast was said,
All the wedding guests were fed.

Frog and Mouse danced one last dance,
Then caught a plane to Paris, France.

And then they were alone again,
One rodent, one amphibian!